ART, YO

Arthur Smith wants to be in the spotlight. But will he be villain or hero?

Sam McBratney taught at a secondary school for a while and is now a primary school teacher. The winner of a Bass Ireland Arts Prize, he has written many books, stories and radio plays for adults and children, including the Walker titles *The Green Kids*, *Flash Eddie and the Big Bad Wolf*, *In Crack Willow Wood*, *Oliver Sundew*, *Tooth Fairy* and *Guess How Much I Love You*. Married with three grown-up children and an ancient tortoise, he lives in County Antrim, Northern Ireland.

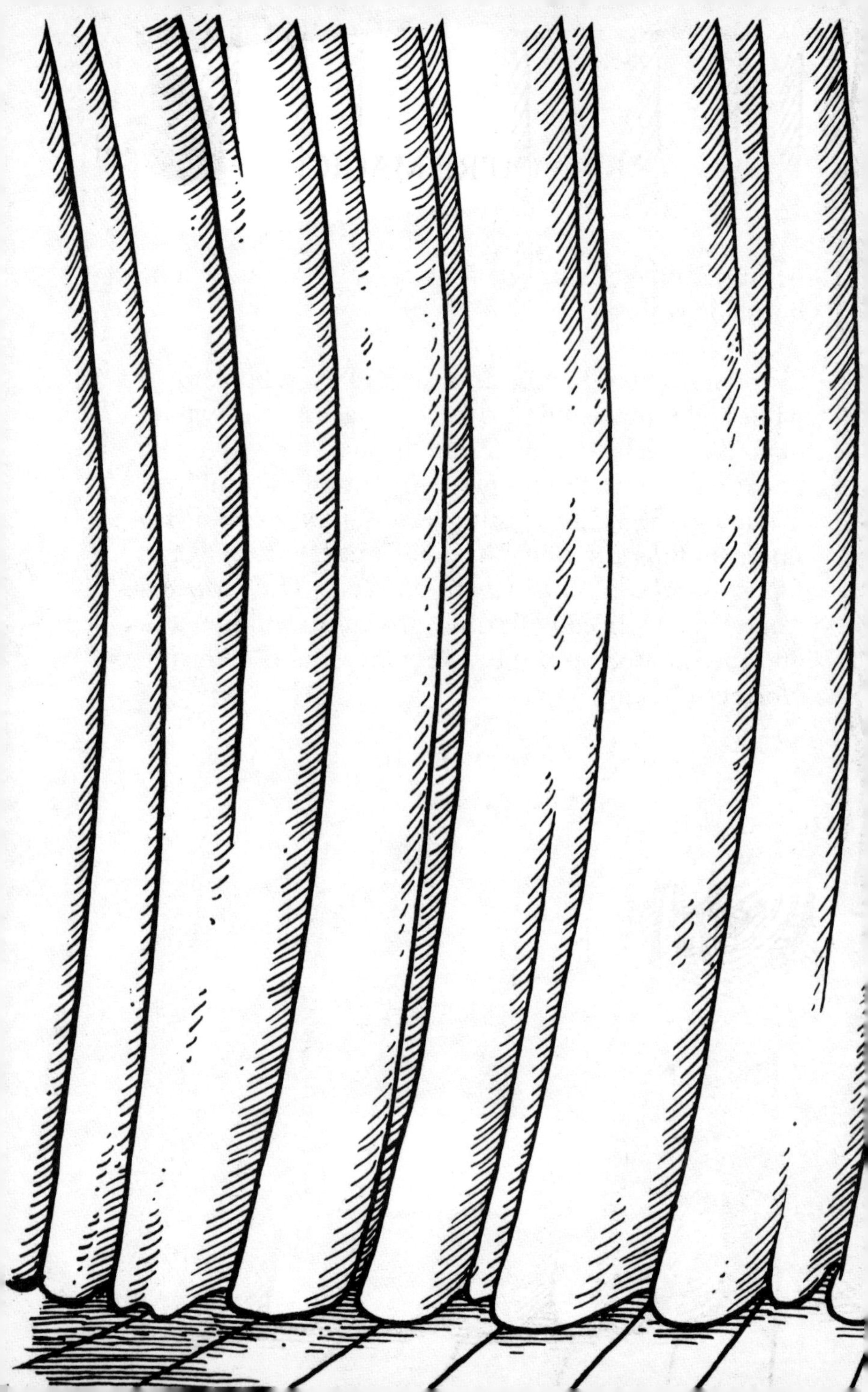

Some other titles

Jolly Roger
by Colin McNaughton

Pappy Mashy
by Kathy Henderson

The Snow Maze
by Jan Mark

Tillie McGillie's Fantastical Chair
by Vivian French

The Unknown Planet
by Jean Ure

SAM McBRATNEY

ART YOU'RE MAGIC!

Illustrations by
Tony Blundell

WALKER BOOKS
AND SUBSIDIARIES
LONDON • BOSTON • SYDNEY

To Oliver and Joe
T.B.

First published 1992 by
Walker Books Ltd, 87 Vauxhall Walk
London SE11 5HJ

This edition published 1994

4 6 8 10 9 7 5

Printed in England

British Library Cataloguing in Publication Data
A catalogue record for this book is available from the British Library.

ISBN 0-7445-3103-9

Contents

Chapter One

Mervyn Magee came to school in a new blue tie.

"I like your tie, Mervyn," everybody said. Even Henrietta Turtle said that she liked Mervyn's tie. Miss Ray, their teacher, said it looked like a lovely big butterfly.

I want a tie like
that, thought Art.

When Art came home from school he talked to his mother in the kitchen.

"Mummy, will you buy me a butterfly tie for round my neck, please? I want a red one."

At that moment his mother was helping Angela, Art's big sister, to whiten her gym shoes on the tiled floor.

"A butterfly tie?" she said. "What on earth is a butterfly tie?"

"He means a bow tie," said Angela. "He wants to look smart for Henrietta Turtle, don't you, Art?"

Angela knew perfectly well that Art didn't like Henrietta Turtle, but Art decided to ignore her.

"I think people would like me better if I had a butterfly tie," he said.

"My sweet angel," said his mother, "everybody likes you as you are. People would adore you if you ran about in rags."

Angela rolled her eyes. "Lay off, Mum, you'll swell his head."

"Well, it's true. And of course you can have a butterfly tie. *If,*" she added, "you promise to keep it good."

Art promised that he would keep it good. And so, when his dad came home that day he found three people waiting for him in the middle of the kitchen – and one of those people was wearing a brand new tie.

"Well, do you notice anything different?" said Mrs Smith.

"By Jove, that's some tie," said Mr Smith.

"Daddy, I picked this tie all by myself. If you want to wear it sometimes, I could lend it to you," shouted Art.

For some reason this made his family laugh. Art tramped cheerfully up the stairs to look at himself in the mirror again.

Chapter Two

Next morning, Art marched into the cloakroom with everybody else in Miss Ray's line. As soon as he took off his coat Henrietta Turtle spotted his new tie.

"Mervyn Magee had one of those ties first," she said, "and you are a copycat, Arthur Smith."

"You shut up," Art said.

Henrietta Turtle certainly wasn't one of his friends and she never would be.

"I won't shut up."

"You're not allowed to talk to me."

"I am allowed if it's true. Copycat!"

You are really making me angry, 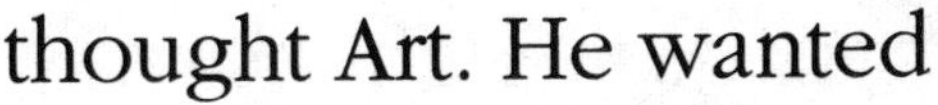thought Art. He wanted to zap Henrietta Turtle and make her howl, but zapping was not allowed in school, so he said, "Shut up, Big Nose."

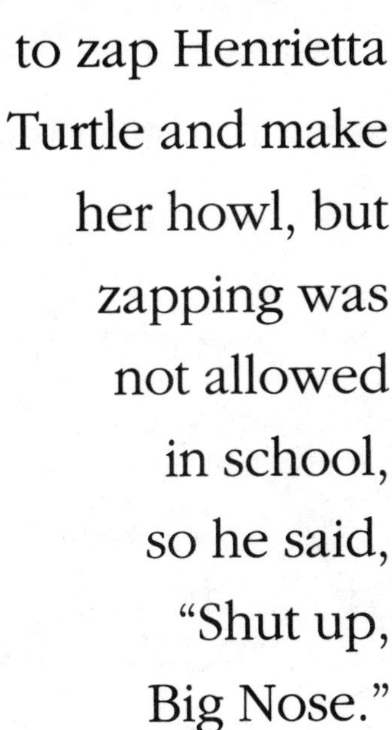

"Don't you call me Big Nose!"

Quite a few people had become interested in this battle of words in the cloakroom and Miss Ray was one of them.

"Henrietta Turtle and Arthur Smith, I want to see both of you in your seats right now."

Art went to his seat thinking how Henrietta Turtle should be moved into somebody else's class. She'd nearly got him into Trouble yet again.

After Miss Ray had taken the register, the class practised for their play. Art was a lion in the play.

Although he roared his loudest, Miss Ray did not say what a good lion he was and she did not say how nice his new tie was.

Art was disappointed and blamed Henrietta Turtle for this.

At break, Art's friend Katy asked him if he wanted to eat some of her yoghurt.

"I wouldn't give him any yoghurt if I was you, Katy," said Henrietta Turtle, "because he's a copycat. Mervyn Magee has a bow tie just like that and he had it first."

Zap, zap! thought Art. Boy, you are really annoying me.

"And another thing," Henrietta Turtle went on, "that tie looks like a big red insect and it's sucking all the blood out of your head."

Art was glad when Henrietta Turtle went away to talk to somebody else.

After break Miss Ray gave her class some number work to do. Everybody had to think hard, especially at Art's table, so there wasn't much noise for a while. Then there was a loud cry.

"Aaaaa! Look what he's done!

He's ruined my special giant rubber and it's my only one!"

Three quick-marching strides brought Miss Ray to the table where Art sat with Mervyn Magee, Katy and Henrietta Turtle. She picked up the giant rubber.

"Who wrote BIG NOSE on this rubber?"

Art sucked his top lip and looked down. Mervyn Magee smiled because he loved Trouble, and Katy chewed her pencil anxiously in case the blame should somehow settle on her.

"YOU DID IT, ARTHUR SMITH!" howled Henrietta Turtle.

It was true, he'd done it. Art's head hung low with shame as Miss Ray walked him to the blackboard with these awful words:

"Well, I didn't think I had any bad children in my class this year, but I was mistaken, wasn't I? You will stand there for five whole minutes, Arthur Smith, so that everybody can

23

see what happens to people who get up to silly nonsense."

And when they practised their play again, Miss Ray wouldn't let him be a lion. Art was not happy. When he got home he found his mother having tea with Katy's mum, who lived next door.

"Well, Art," said Katy's mum, "did you dazzle everybody with your new ... what do you call it?"

"Butterfly tie," said Mrs Smith.

Art was no fool, he saw them smiling at him. "I'm going to zap Henrietta Turtle," he cried, and his eyes were fierce and blue. "I'm going to zap her head off!"

That made the mothers stop smiling. Art didn't care. Up the stairs he went to crawl under the bed and lie there in the peace and quiet with some of his toys.

Chapter Three

All the world seemed far away as Art lay curled up in the half-dark, thinking how this tie, the one round his neck, was a stupid tie. I don't want it any more, he decided.

A familiar sound reached his ears.

In the garden next door, Katy's yappy dog was barking. Art began to bark too, as if he understood dog-talk.

And then a wonderful idea came into his head and all of a sudden he knew what to do with his tie – the very thing! As fast as he could go Art raced down the stairs and out into the garden to where the fence was lowest. Peanuts looked up at him, wagging his tail.

"Yappy dog," Art called quietly.

"Rrrrrruf!"

"I've got something for you here," said Art, climbing over the fence into Katy's garden.

Yappy dog Peanuts had never seen a butterfly tie before and he didn't seem to want one – Art had some trouble fitting it round his neck.

At last the job was done, and what a difference that tie made to tatty old

Peanuts! Below the straggly whiskers that poked about in the dirt all day could now be seen a splendid dash of butterfly-shaped colour.

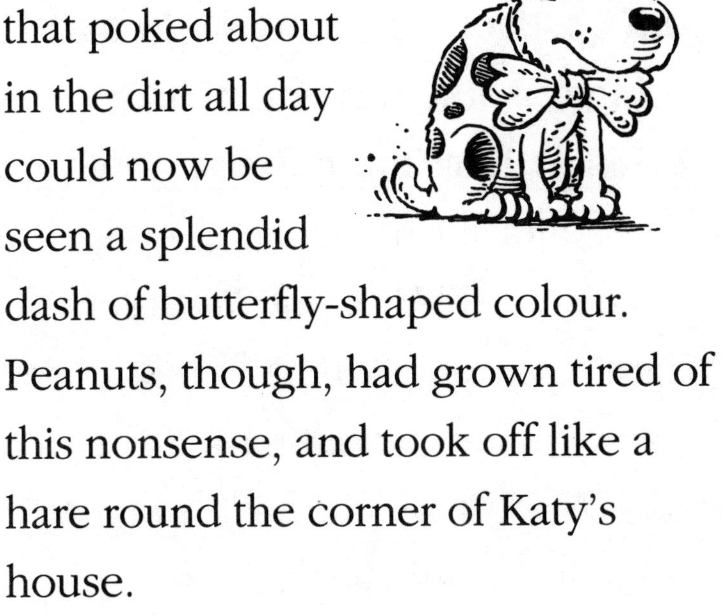

Peanuts, though, had grown tired of this nonsense, and took off like a hare round the corner of Katy's house.

And the butterfly tie went with him!

Ding-dong! ding-dong!

Art heard the doorbell plainly from upstairs, where he sat in bed talking to some furry animals.

"Art. Arthur Smith! Come down those stairs at once."

Dad's voice! Was this Trouble? When Art went into the living-room he saw the red tie dangling from his dad's hand. It was dirty; it hung in tatters; it was all chewed up.

"Jeepers, Dad!" said Angela. "Is that the new tie?"

"It *was*," said Mr Smith.

"The twit must have been wearing it round his welly boot," cried Angela.

Don't you dare call me a twit, thought Art. But he could see that this was Trouble, all right.

"A little while ago," said Mr Smith, "Katy's mum saw Peanuts the dog down at the shops with something round his neck that looked like a tie. That can't be *Art's* tie, she said to herself, Art is wearing his new tie. But it *was* his tie. She found it later on the back step. And here it is!"

"You stuck your new tie on that scruffy *beast*?" cried Angela.

"I thought it was his birthday," Art mumbled.

"NUTS!" cried Angela. "Dogs do not have birthdays. One dog's day is like any other, and they can't count. There's something wrong with your brain, Arthur Smith."

"You stop talking to me," said Art.

But there was plenty of talking to be done and Mr Smith did most of it as he trailed Art back to bed. He was still talking about the price of clothes, and about the boys and girls in the world who couldn't afford to buy food never mind new ties, as he tucked Art in for the night.

Mum came in to say night-night, and held up the lion's tail she'd made for him. "You'd better not forget this in the morning," she said, and put out the light.

I don't want to go to school and I don't want to be a lion and everybody's cross with me, thought Art. People blame me for everything. How many times had Miss Ray smiled at him all day? Not once. Art reached out an arm and dragged Big Bendy into bed with him, his true friend, and lay down to sleep. Was it true, he wondered, that dogs didn't have birthdays?

Chapter Four

Next morning Art went off to school with his lion's tail carefully folded up in his school bag.

This was an important Friday morning because Miss Ray's class were putting on a play for the other infant classes. Quite a few mothers were coming to watch it too, including Art's.

The play was a very good story – Art was sure that people would enjoy it. Once there was a bad king and this bad king put Daniel into the cave with lions. He thought the lions would eat Daniel, but they didn't. God sent an angel – Katy – and the angel made the lions close their mouths. They couldn't hurt Daniel, and he was safe.

So, at ten past nine, the children from the other classes came out of their rooms and walked down to the Hall. Here they sat in rows and waited for Miss Ray's class to come in and do their play.

The people in the Hall didn't know that there was a problem. Ernie wasn't here. He was at home in bed. Miss Ray had no Daniel!

"What am I going to *do*?" she said to Katy's mum, who was there to pin on Katy's angel wings. "How can I have a play about Daniel without a *Daniel*; why did he pick *this* Friday to get the chicken-pox?"

"Maybe you could do the play next week," said Katy's mum.

All the children began to groan.

Then Miss Ray felt someone prodding her with a lion's mask.

"I can be Daniel," said a voice – she looked down, and there was Art.

NOTICE

"Can you? Can you really? Do you know the words?"

"I know everybody's words," said Art.

"He does, Miss Ray," said Katy, "he knows everybody's words. He said them all to me when we were going home from school."

"Then we'll try it!" cried Miss Ray. "Quick, get him dressed."

There wasn't a moment to lose because everybody in the Hall was waiting. Katy's mum took off Art's tail and dressed him up in Daniel's clothes – a towel for his head and a stripy pyjama top.

Then all the lions and the bad king and Daniel and the angel hurried up the corridor as fast as they could go.

Chapter Five

When Art got up on the stage in front of everybody that Friday morning he waved to his mum to make sure she knew he wasn't a lion any more.

And then the play began.

The best moment came when the bad king pushed Daniel among the lions, who walked round in a circle and began to roar. Art looked down at all the children who were watching, and he knew what they were thinking – they were thinking that he would soon be eaten.

Now it was time for Katy to say her words. She had to tell the lions to close their mouths and leave Daniel alone.

But she didn't. Katy couldn't. She was afraid to speak in front of all those people.

The lions were going wild! Henrietta Turtle, who was definitely the best lion, was roaring her head off and waving her mask about. The play was going to be ruined if Katy didn't speak!

Art walked across the stage and put an arm round her shoulder. "You'd better shut them up or Henrietta Turtle is going to eat me," he said.

Katy looked at Henrietta and saw that this was true. She waved an arm in the air – a very angry angel.

"Shut your mouth, Henrietta Turtle!" she called out. Her words worked like magic.

Henrietta Turtle closed her lips and sucked them into her mouth, as if she had no teeth. Then she stuck her hands under her armpits to show that her fierce paws didn't work, either. All the lions did the same and they looked like pet mice. Daniel was saved and the play was over.

Everybody clapped and clapped. Art's mum was one of those who clapped the longest and he could see that she'd forgotten all the trouble caused by that stupid tie.

In the corridor Miss Ray swept Art off his feet and gave him quite a strong cuddle.

"Arthur Smith, you are magic," she said. "I have never seen a more wonderful Daniel and I think you're just great."

Art hoped that Henrietta Turtle was listening.